THE BOO CREW NEEDS YOU!

Words by Vicky Fang

Pictures by Saoirse Lou

SOURCEBOOKS jabberwocky

Guess what's happening tonight...
Halloween! What a delight!

BC

We'll make sure it goes just right!
Love, The Boo Crew ♥

Could you check that it's all good?
Look around the neighborhood?
TURN THE PAGE now, if you would
for the Boo Crew!

What a sight! It's a fright!
This will ruin our great night!
There's disasters left and right!
It's a zoo, too!

Nothing's going right at all!
Will this wreck the Monster Ball?

Quick,
PRESS HERE
to make a call
for the Boo Crew!

Ring-a-ling! Here's the gang:
This is Luna, Bones, and Fang.

What's the problem?

Someone rang?

We're the Boo Crew!

When the monsters see the mess,
they are overcome with stress!
Will you help them?

Please
SHOUT "YES!"

to the Boo Crew!

Yay, hooray! You're a team!

Wait a minute, is that steam?

Did you hear somebody scream?

Come on, Boo Crew!

That's it, Boo Crew!

What's that shouting now? Oh no!

Well done, Boo Crew!

Wait, there's more? What is that?
It's a mischievous black cat.
All the pumpkins have gone splat!
They need Boo Glue!

Okay, gluing should be fun.

TAP each pumpkin, one by one...

Turn the page when you are done...

Hooray, Boo Crew!

Job well done. Take a break.
There's an awful lot at stake.

Go,
go,
Boo
Crew!

There it is! My oh my,
it's a spell that's gone awry.
Spooky Hall is on its side!
Oh dear, Boo Crew.

Yes, that's it! That's a rope!

Clap your hands to give them hope!

CLAP, CLAP, CLAP

until we—

This is great! Oh, but wait... Now we're in this sideways state.

SHAKE the book and TURN us straight!

Nice one, Boo Crew!

Yes, it worked. It's a win!

Let the Monster Ball begin!

Come in, Boo Crew!

Now the ball can go as planned,

and the evening will be grand!

Guess we all could use a hand—

even the Boo Crew.

You have saved the monster fest!

PAT your back! I'm impressed.

Yes, the Boo Crew is the best!

To my writing crew, Christine and Faith.
—VF

For my Josh, who loves all things spooky.
—SL

The illustrations were created both traditionally with gouache paint and digitally using Procreate on a tablet.

Published by Sourcebooks Jabberwocky, an imprint of Sourcebooks Kids
P.O. Box 4410, Naperville, Illinois 60567–4410
(630) 961-3900
sourcebookskids.com

Cataloging-in-Publication Data is on file with the Library of Congress.

Source of Production: 1010 Printing Asia Limited, Kwun Tong, Hong Kong, China
Date of Production: January 2023
Run Number: 5029480

Printed and bound in China.
OGP 10 9 8 7 6 5 4 3 2 1